Sports Illustrated Kids: Leg

T0012453

CRISTIANO
RONALDO

VS.

LIONEL
MESSI

SOCCER LEGENDS
FACE OFF

by Karen Bischer

CAPSTONE PRESS
a capstone imprint

Published by Capstone Press, an imprint of Capstone
1710 Roe Crest Drive, North Mankato, Minnesota 56003
capstonepub.com

Library of Congress Cataloging-in-Publication Data
Names: Bischer, Karen, author.
Title: Cristiano Ronaldo vs. Lionel Messi : soccer legends face off / by Karen Bischer.
Other titles: Cristiano Ronaldo versus Lionel Messi
Description: North Mankato, MN : Capstone Press, [2025] | Series: Sports illustrated kids. Legend vs. legend | Includes bibliographical references and index. | Audience: Ages 9–11 | Audience: Grades 4–6 | Summary: "Cristiano Ronaldo and Lionel Messi are soccer superstars! Between the two, Ronaldo has more career goals, but Messi leads in career assists. So which one is the all-time best? Young readers can decide for themselves by comparing the fantastic feats and stunning stats of two legendary pro soccer players"— Provided by publisher.
Identifiers: LCCN 2023054264 (print) | LCCN 2023054265 (ebook) | ISBN 9781669079620 (hardcover) | ISBN 9781669079576 (paperback) | ISBN 9781669079583 (pdf) | ISBN 9781669079606 (kindle edition) | ISBN 9781669079590 (epub)
Subjects: LCSH: Ronaldo, Cristiano, 1985-—Juvenile literature. | Messi, Lionel, 1987-—Juvenile literature. | Soccer players—Portugal--Biography—Juvenile literature. | Soccer players—Argentina—Biography—Juvenile literature.
Classification: LCC GV942.7.R626 B57 2025 (print) | LCC GV942.7.R626 (ebook) | DDC 796.334092 [B]—dc23/eng/20231130
LC record available at https://lccn.loc.gov/2023054264
LC ebook record available at https://lccn.loc.gov/2023054265

Editorial Credits
Editor: Christopher Harbo; Designer: Sarah Bennett; Media Researcher: Svetlana Zhurkin; Production Specialist: Katy LaVigne

Image Credits
Associated Press: Emilio Morenatti, 17; Getty Images: Al Bello, 10, Alex Caparros, 21, Carmen Mandato, 29, Gonzalo Arroyo Moreno, 26, Jean Catuffe, 24, Lars Baron, 15, 19, Matthias Hangst, 14, NurPhoto/Xavier Bonilla, 16, PA Images/Mike Egerton, 18, Real Madrid/Angel Martinez, 11; Newscom: Action Plus/Pierpaolo Piciucco, 12, Action Plus/Sports Images, 25, Cal Sport Media/David Klein, 22, EFE/Javier Lizon, 20, Image of Sport/Jon Endow, 13, SIPA/ Chine Nouvelle/Xinhua/Xiao Yijiu, 6, Xinhua News Agency/Henri Szwarc, 27, ZUMA Press/star-images, 23; Shutterstock: Christian Bertrand, 4, Dmytro Larin, cover (left), imagestockdesign, 28, Maciej Rogowski Photo, 7, Marco Iacobucci Epp, cover (right), saicle (background), cover and throughout, Victor Velter, 5, 9, Vlad1988, 8

CONTENTS

* * * All stats current through the 2022–2023 season. * * *
Words in **bold** appear in the glossary.

Soccer Legends Face Off!

Cristiano Ronaldo and Lionel Messi are two of the world's best soccer players. Their amazing skills thrill fans and help their teams win. Ronaldo is known for his power. Messi is known for his ball control. But which player is the best? Let's find out!

Cristiano Ronaldo

Lionel Messi

THE MATCHUP	Born	Country
Ronaldo	February 5, 1985	Portugal
Messi	June 24, 1987	Argentina

Height and Speed

Both Messi and Ronaldo use their height and speed to make big plays! Messi's smaller size helps him stay balanced. In the 2022 **World Cup**, his fastest clocked speed was 19.5 miles (31.4 kilometers) per hour. Ronaldo's extra inches help him jump high. His top World Cup speed was 19.9 miles (32.1 km) per hour.

Messi controls the ball during the final match in the 2022 World Cup.

Ronaldo kicks the ball in the air.

THE MATCHUP	Height	Fastest World Cup Speed
Messi	5 feet, 7 inches (170 centimeters)	19.5 miles (31.4 km) per hour
Ronaldo	6 feet, 2 inches (188 cm)	19.9 miles (32.1 km) per hour

Matches Played

Messi and Ronaldo always show up to play.

Each has been in more than 1,000 **matches**!

So far, Ronaldo has played in 1,176 matches

with five pro teams and Portugal's national team.

But Messi isn't far behind. He has played in

1,036 matches with three pro teams and

Argentina's national team.

Ronaldo playing for Portugal

Messi playing for Paris Saint-Germain

THE MATCHUP	Matches Played	Teams
Ronaldo	1,176	Sporting Lisbon, Manchester United, Real Madrid, Juventus, Al-Nassr, and Portugal
Messi	1,036	FC Barcelona, Paris Saint-Germain, Inter Miami, and Argentina

Goals

Messi and Ronaldo are scoring sensations. Messi has 808 goals. One of his most famous came in his first match for Inter Miami in 2023. He scored the match-winning goal! Ronaldo has 838 goals. In 2018, he scored on a thrilling **bicycle kick** for Real Madrid. It even made the other team's fans cheer!

Messi after scoring his first goal for Inter Miami

Ronaldo kicking an overhead goal for Real Madrid

THE MATCHUP	Goals
Messi	808
Ronaldo	838

Assists

Scoring goals takes teamwork. Both Messi and Ronaldo are masters at **assists**. As of 2023, Ronaldo has 236 career assists. But Messi is the all-time assist king with 357.

Ronaldo celebrating after an assist

Inter Miami's Messi with his teammates after an assist

THE MATCHUP	Assists
Ronaldo	236
Messi	357

UEFA Performances

Messi and Ronaldo have played in the **UEFA** Champions League. This league is made up of teams from across Europe. Ronaldo is the league's all-time top scorer with 140 goals. He won five UEFA **championships**. Messi comes in second with 129 goals. He won three UEFA championships.

Messi scores a goal for Paris Saint-Germain during a UEFA Champions League match.

Ronaldo scores a goal for Juventus in a UEFA Champions League match.

THE MATCHUP	UEFA Goals	UEFA Championships
Ronaldo	140	5
Messi	129	3

La Liga Performances

Messi and Ronaldo both played in La Liga, Spain's top soccer **division**. Messi won 10 La Liga championships with FC Barcelona. Ronaldo won two championships with Real Madrid. Messi is also La Liga's top scorer with 474 goals. Ronaldo is second best with 311 goals.

Messi scoring a goal for FC Barcelona

Ronaldo playing for Real Madrid

THE MATCHUP	La Liga Championships	La Liga Goals
Messi	10	474
Ronaldo	2	311

Hat Tricks

Messi and Ronaldo are **hat trick** hot shots. They have scored three or more goals in a match more than 100 times combined. As of 2023, Messi had 57 hat tricks. But Ronaldo led with 62.

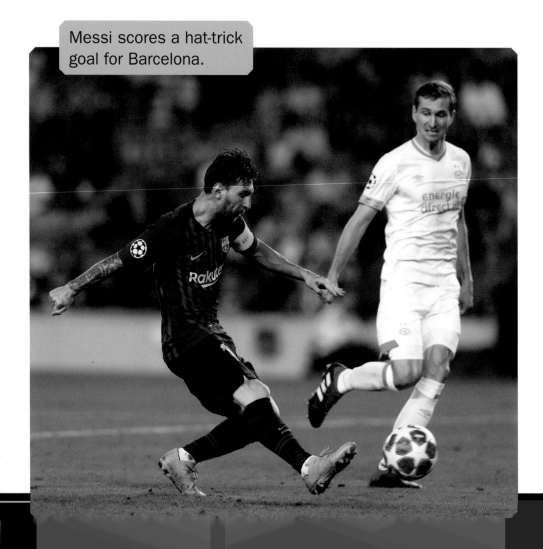

Messi scores a hat-trick goal for Barcelona.

Ronaldo kicks his third goal during a match for Real Madrid.

THE MATCHUP	Hat Tricks
Messi	57
Ronaldo	62

El Clásico Performances

FC Barcelona and Real Madrid are big **rivals** in Spain. When the teams play each other, it's known as El Clásico. Messi has played in El Clásico matches 45 times. He has scored 26 goals. Ronaldo has had 18 goals in 30 El Clásico matches.

Messi (10) and his teammates celebrate his goal against Real Madrid.

Ronaldo's teammates celebrate his second goal in a match against FC Barcelona.

THE MATCHUP	El Clásico Matches	El Clásico Goals
Messi	45	26
Ronaldo	30	18

World Cup Performances

Every four years, soccer teams represent their countries in the World Cup. Playing for Portugal, Ronaldo has eight goals in 22 World Cup matches. Messi has 13 goals in 26 matches for Argentina. In 2022, Messi's team won the whole **tournament**!

Ronaldo scores his first goal during the 2022 World Cup.

Messi (with the trophy) and his teammates celebrate their win in the 2022 World Cup.

THE MATCHUP	World Cup Matches	World Cup Goals	World Cup Wins
Ronaldo	22	8	0
Messi	26	13	1

Match-Winning Goals

What is the most important goal of a match? The one that wins the game! As of 2023, Messi had scored 172 match-winning goals. But Ronaldo had him beat. He had scored 206 match-winners!

Messi kicks a match-winning goal for Paris Saint-Germain.

Ronaldo scores the winning goal for Juventus from a penalty kick.

THE MATCHUP	Match-Winning Goals
Messi	172
Ronaldo	206

Ballon d'Or Awards

Messi and Ronaldo have taken home a lot of trophies. The Ballon d'Or is one of soccer's biggest awards. It honors the best player in the world. Ronaldo has won this award five times. Messi has won it seven times.

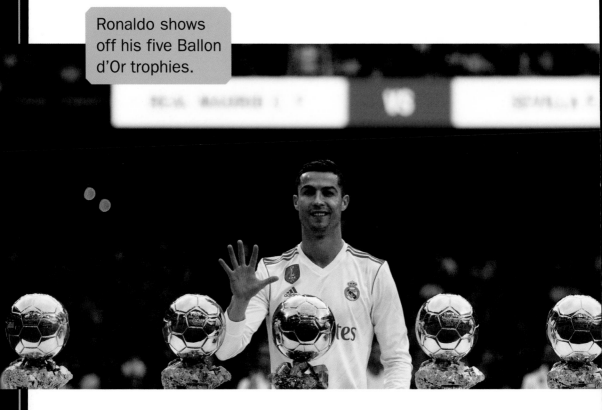

Ronaldo shows off his five Ballon d'Or trophies.

Messi with his seventh
Ballon d'Or trophy

THE MATCHUP	Ballon d'Or Awards
Ronaldo	5
Messi	7

Who Is the Best?

Messi and Ronaldo are soccer superstars! Messi has more assists, but Ronaldo has more hat tricks. Ronaldo has more goals, but Messi has won a World Cup. Both help their teams win and keep fans on the edge of their seats.

Who is the best player? You make the call!

Cristiano Ronaldo

Lionel Messi

Glossary

assist (uh-SIST)—a pass that leads to a goal by a teammate

bicycle kick (BYE-si-kuhl KIK)—a kick in which a player jumps backward into the air and kicks the ball when it is over their head

championship (CHAM-pee-uhn-ship)—a contest or final game of a series that determines which team will be the overall winner

division (duh-VIH-zhuhn)—a group of teams in a certain category for a competition

hat trick (HAT TRIK)—when a player scores three goals in a match

match (MACH)—a game or sporting competition

rival (RYE-vuhl)—a person or team another person or team competes against

tournament (TUR-nuh-muhnt)—a series of matches between several players or teams, ending in one winner

UEFA (YU-AY-FAH)—short for the Union of European Football Associations

World Cup (WURLD CUP)—a soccer competition held every four years in which teams from around the world compete against each other

Read More

Abdo, Kenny. *Lionel Messi.* Minneapolis: Abdo Zoom, 2023.

Buckley, James Jr. *Who Is Cristiano Ronaldo?* New York: Penguin Workshop, 2022.

Wagner, Zelda. *Soccer Superstars.* Minneapolis: Lerner Publications, 2025.

Internet Sites

FIFA: The Home of Football
fifa.com

Messi vs Ronaldo: All Time Career Goals and Stats
messivsronaldo.app

Soccer: SI Kids
sikids.com/tag/soccer

Index

About the Author

Photo by K. Bischer

Karen Bischer is a writer and New Jersey resident who loves watching sports, especially baseball. When she's not cheering on her beloved New York Yankees, you can find her playing with (or being bossed around by) her cat, Clarence, and dog, Brandy.